S0-AZO-346

ILLINOIS TEXTBOOK
LOAN PROGRAM
FY _____

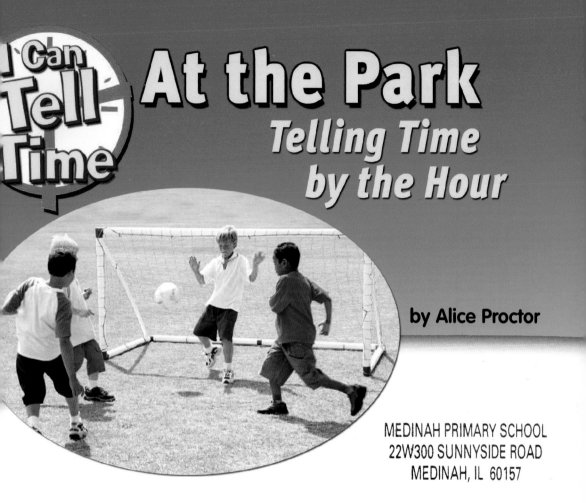

I Can Tell Time

At the Park
Telling Time
by the Hour

by Alice Proctor

MEDINAH PRIMARY SCHOOL
22W300 SUNNYSIDE ROAD
MEDINAH, IL 60157

WEEKLY READER®
PUBLISHING

Math and Curriculum Consultant:
Debra Voege, M.A.,
Science and Math Curriculum Resource Teacher

Please visit our web site at: www.garethstevens.com
For a free color catalog describing our list of high-quality books,
call 1-800-542-2595 (USA) or 1-800-387-3178 (Canada).

Library of Congress Cataloging-in-Publication Data

Proctor, Alice, 1967-
    At the park: telling time by the hour / Alice Proctor.
        p. cm. — (I can tell time)
    ISBN-10: 0-8368-8389-6 — ISBN-13: 978-0-8368-8389-3 (lib. bdg.)
    ISBN-10: 0-8368-8394-2 — ISBN-13: 978-0-8368-8394-7 (softcover)
    1. Time—Juvenile literature.   2. Day—Juvenile literature.
    3. Parks—Juvenile literature.   I. Title.
    QB209.5.P764   2007
    529'.7—dc22   2007017437

This North American edition first published in 2008 by
Weekly Reader® Books
An imprint of Gareth Stevens Publishing
1 Reader's Digest Road
Pleasantville, NY 10570-7000 USA

This U.S. edition copyright © 2008 by Gareth Stevens, Inc. Original
edition copyright © 2007 by ticktock Entertainment Ltd. First published
in Great Britain in 2007 by ticktock Media Ltd., Unit 2, Orchard Business
Centre, North Farm Road, Tunbridge Wells, Kent, TN2 3XF, United Kingdom.

Gareth Stevens series editor: Dorothy L. Gibbs
Gareth Stevens graphic design and cover design: Dave Kowalski
Gareth Stevens art direction: Tammy West

Picture credits: (t=top, b=bottom, c=center, l=left, r=right)
Alamy: 11. Banana Stock: 1, 6t, 13b, 16, 17t, 19b. Gettyimages/Michael
Wildsmith: 8bl. Jupiter Images (Banana Stock): 18, 19t. Photolibrary/Creatas:
10tl. Shutterstock: cover, 4, 5, 9tl, 13t, 14, 23 all, 24br. Superstock: 9br, 10br,
12, 15b, 17b. Ticktock Media Archive: 6b, 7 both, 8bc, 15t, 21, 22 all, 24bl.

Every effort has been made to trace the copyright holders for the pictures used
in this book. We apologize in advance for any unintentional omissions and would
be pleased to insert the appropriate acknowledgements in any subsequent edition.

All rights reserved. No part of this book may be reproduced, stored in
a retrieval system, or transmitted in any form or by any means, electronic,
mechanical, photocopying, recording, or otherwise, without the prior written
permission of the copyright holder.

Printed in the United States of America

1 2 3 4 5 6 7 8 9 11 10 09 08 07

Contents

Glossary words are printed in **boldface** type in the text.

Times of the Day

A day is 24 hours long. It has a daytime and a nighttime. The sky is light during the daytime. The sky is dark during the nighttime.

Morning and Afternoon

Morning is the first part of the **day**. It starts at 12 **o'clock midnight**. Part of the morning is dark, and you are still asleep.

Daytime starts when the Sun comes up. Most of the time you are awake is during the daytime.

Morning ends at **noon**, or 12 o'clock. At this time of the day, the Sun is high in the sky.

The next part of the day is called **afternoon**. It lasts from noon until about dinnertime.

4

Evening and Night

Evening is next. It is the time of the day when the Sun is going down, and the sky is starting to get dark. As the Sun sets, the sky gets darker and darker.

After the Sun sets, it is **night**. The sky is dark now, and you can see the Moon and stars.

You sleep through most of the night. While you are asleep, the next morning starts — at 12 o'clock midnight.

What time of the day is it now?

Telling Time

Sunday is my birthday. I am having a party at the park. My friends will be there at noon.

Let's find out how clocks work so we will know when my friends are coming.

Clocks with Hands

Many clocks have two hands. The little hand is called the **hour** hand. It shows us what hour of the day it is.

The big hand is called the **minute** hand. It shows us how many minutes it is before or after the hour.

minute hand

hour hand

What time is it?

Each hour of the day starts when the big hand is pointing at the 12.

On this clock, the big hand is pointing at the 12. The little hand is pointing at the 2. The time is exactly 2 o'clock!

Digital Clocks

Digital clocks do not have hands. They show the time using two numbers. The first number shows the hour. The second number shows how many minutes it is past the hour.

This digital watch shows 0 minutes past the hour of 8. The time is exactly 8 o'clock!

The big hand on the twelve always means "o'clock."

Time to Get Up!

It is Sunday morning. Today is my birthday! I can't wait to have my party at the park.

Starting the Day

7 o'clock

My alarm clock rings, but I am already awake. I jump out of bed and get dressed. It is sunny outside so I put on shorts and a T-shirt.

I hope my friends remember to come to my party today!

Breakfast Time

I eat a healthy birthday breakfast. Cereal and orange juice are my favorite breakfast foods.

8 o'clock

Look! The mailman is here. He has eight birthday cards for me!

The mailman gives me a package, too. It's a birthday present from Uncle Bob — some toy cars and a Frisbee.

When is your birthday?

9

My Birthday Morning

Grandma and Grandpa are here. They are coming to my party, too.

A Special Present

9 o'clock

Grandma and Grandpa tell me they have a special present for me outside. I rush out the door to see it.

Wow! It's a new bike! I want to ride my new bike to the park.

Time to Go!

10 o'clock

The park is close to our house, but Mom and Grandma and Grandpa will go there in the car. They have a lot of things to carry for the party.

Dad says he will ride his bike with me to the park.

Come on, Dad. Let's go!

Always wear a safety helmet when you ride your bike!

My Party at the Park

It is going to be a warm, sunny day. Mom finds a shady spot in the park for my party.

Setting Up

11 o'clock

Mom and Grandma set up a picnic table for the party. Look at all the yummy food!

We are going to play games, too. I hope I win a prize!

Party Time!

12 o'clock

It is noon at last! It is time for my party to start. My friends Justin and Michael are the first ones here.

Treasure Hunt

The first game we play is a treasure hunt! Justin finds the treasure. It is chocolate coins! He shares them with everyone.

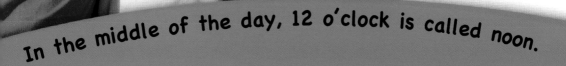

In the middle of the day, 12 o'clock is called noon.

13

Cake and Presents

Now it is time for lunch. We are having a party picnic. We have sandwiches, fruit, and lemonade.

Time for Cake

1 o'clock
Grandma lights the candles on my birthday cake.

After everyone sing "Happy Birthday," I blow out the candles. Then we all have a piece of cake. It's yummy!

More Presents!

My friends brought me more birthday presents. One of them is this awesome watch. I am so lucky. Now I can tell time with my own wristwatch! I thank everyone for all the great presents.

Another Party Game

2 o'clock

I look at my watch. The time is 2 o'clock. We still have 2 hours before my party is over. Let's play baseball!

What is your favorite party game?

Afternoon Fun

We played baseball for an hour. It sure made us thirsty. After a cold drink, we are ready for more fun.

Time for Soccer

3 o'clock

My friends want to play with my new soccer ball. Soccer is my favorite game.

The Party Is Over

4 o'clock

It is time for my friends to go home now. We sure had a lot of fun this afternoon!

One Last Game

Dad offers to clean up so Mom and I can play with my new Frisbee. Grandma and Grandpa help Dad put away the food and pick up all the litter. We do not want to leave a mess in the park.

fternoon is the part of the day between lunch and dinner.

17

The End of the Day

I am too tired to ride my bike home. Dad puts our bikes on the back of Mom's car, then we all ride home together.

Dinnertime

5 o'clock

By the time we get home, the Sun is low in the sky. It is almost time for dinner.

Dad makes a special dinner for my birthday. He knows how much I like pasta!

Time for a Treat

6 o'clock

Mom and Dad surprise me with a special birthday treat. We have ice cream sundaes for dessert!

Bedtime

7 o'clock

After a bath, I go to bed. Dad comes to read me a story, but I am already asleep!

What time do you go to bed?

Time Facts

When it is daytime where you are, it is nighttime on the other side of the world.

Light or Dark?

Earth spins around like a top. As it **rotates**, or turns, only one side at a time gets light from the Sun.

If Earth did not rotate, one side would always have daytime. The other side would always have nighttime.

Is it daytime or nighttime now where you are?

Times to Remember

Try these fun puzzles to see what you remember about time.

What time is it?
Look at these clocks.
Can you match each time with the right clock?

| 8 o'clock | 1 o'clock | 3 o'clock |

Day or Night?
Which of these things would you see during the day?
Which ones would you see at night?

What time of day is it now?

Glossary

afternoon – the part of a day between 12 o'clock noon and the time when the Sun starts to set

day – a period of time that starts and ends at 12 o'clock midnight and lasts 24 hours

evening – the part of a day between afternoon and night, when the Sun is setting

hour – a measure of time that equals 60 minutes. Each day has 24 hours.

midnight – the 12 o'clock hour in the middle of the night

minute – a measure of time that equals 60 seconds. Each hour has 60 minutes.

morning – the part of a day between 12 o'clock midnight and 12 o'clock noon

night – the part of a day when it is dark outside and when most people sleep

noon – the 12 o'clock hour in the middle of the day

o'clock – any hour of the day when the big hand on a clock is pointing exactly at the 12. The little hand shows what hour it is.

rotates – turns around and around, spinning like a top

Answers

1 o'clock   3 o'clock   8 o'clock   daytime   nighttime

24